MRS. MACKENZIE'S CANDLE

OTHER BOOKS BY BRYAN WEBB

Hungry Devils and Other Tales from Vanuatu

The Sons of Cannibals

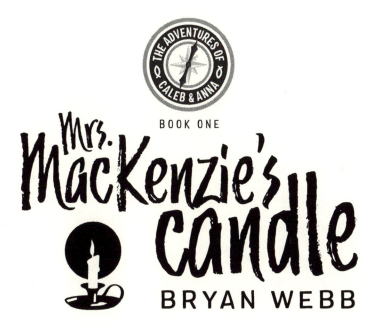

THE ADVENTURES OF CALEB & ANNA

BOOK ONE

Mrs. MacKenzie's candle

BRYAN WEBB

NATORA PRESS
NEOSHO, MISSOURI

Printed in the United States of America

26 25 24 23 22   1 2 3 4 5

ISBN 978-0-9862714-1-0

Illustrated by Forrest Morgan

Book design by Dawn M. Brandon (dawn@ravensbrook.net)

All Scripture quotations are taken from The Holy Bible, King James Version.

*To Olfala George, who introduced me to
Big Bay and all its wonders*

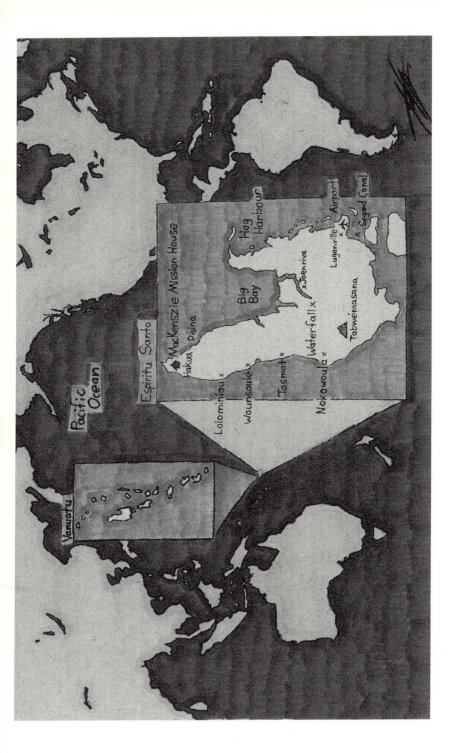

PROLOGUE AND ARRIVAL

May 18

CALEB GRISTMAN stared out the scratched window of the Twin Otter plane and tried his best to stay awake. He wanted to be the first in his family to spot Espiritu Santo, the island that would be their home for the next two months. In the seat beside him, his twelve-year-old sister, Anna, was intently studying papers from the "Mission: Vanuatu" packet Mom had created to help them learn about the country when she and Dad had dramatically revealed where their

1

family would be going. He recognized the Y-shaped group of eighty-five islands—an archipelago, Mom had called it—and the star representing the capital (Port Vila, as he recalled) on the island of Efate.

Caleb congratulated himself on remembering the details despite his typical dislike for boring facts and figures. Memorizing facts was fine for kids like Anna. She liked knowing that the largest island, Santo Espiritu, was fifty miles wide and seventy-five miles long, with a population of forty thousand. Although he knew the names of a few of the biggest islands—Santo, Efate, and Tanna—he wouldn't be surprised if Anna could rattle off the names of all eighty-five! She had been so impressed to learn that 120 different languages were spoken in the islands and was worried about how they would ever be able to communicate with any of the people there. She seemed intrigued that Granny Gristman remembered when Vanuatu was called New Hebrides before it gained independence in 1980.

Such facts bored Caleb, although he had been interested to learn that he would receive 114 vatu, the local currency, for every U.S. dollar he exchanged. That sounded like a good deal to him. What had interested Caleb as they had studied Vanuatu was the stories of people—early missionaries like John Williams, James Harris, and J. Noble MacKenzie—and their exciting adventures as they brought the gospel to a strange new land. Williams and Harris had even been martyred—attacked, killed, and *eaten*, no less—by cannibals on the island of Erromango. Their brave stories had inspired many more missionaries to accept the challenge of evangelizing Vanuatu, including the MacKenzies. Now those were interesting stories!

But for some reason, the story that interested him most was the story of J. Noble MacKenzie, the man who, more than a hundred years ago, had started the first churches among the tribes living on the west coast of Santo. He had also translated the Bible and many hymns into the local language. It was to these same villages, on the west coast of Santo, that the Gristmans would be going. The idea of retracing the important missionary's footsteps, with Dad preaching revival services in each village reached by Mr. MacKenzie, appealed to something deep inside Caleb. It's what made him eager to go to Vanuatu.

In fact, Caleb planned to become part of the story himself. As a special project, he planned to map out the homestead of MacKenzie and his wife, Maggie, at Hakua. He would take GPS readings at key points on the property, photograph the site as it was now, and locate and identify any artifacts remaining from the first mission house. The thought was exciting enough to rouse him—at least for the moment—from his boredom during their seemingly endless flight.

The noise of the engines droned on and on, and the thick tropical air swirled in through the one-inch cracks around the door. Try as he might to keep his eyes open and take in the sights, his head kept bumping against the window as he nodded off.

Two days earlier, at the airport in Dallas, they had said goodbye to Granny and Grandpa Gristman. Granny had hugged them over and over and fussed over them as if they were never coming back. She had made Caleb and Anna promise to write a detailed email every day. After checking in a mountain of luggage—Caleb was sure it was far more than they needed—they had said their goodbyes and headed off on their adventure.

Actually, now that he thought back on it, there had been a little delay getting the adventure underway. Who knew that you had to remove your shoes, take off your belt, empty your pockets of coins, and take your pen out before you could get through the metal detector?

Finally, on his fourth try, barefoot and holding his pants up to keep them from falling (Mom had insisted he would grow into them), he'd made it past the metal detector. He was thankful that he had remembered to slip his Swiss Army knife into his checked bag at the last minute. He would have felt sick if security had taken it away from him.

What he hadn't anticipated was how tiring it would be to travel for two days. When he'd mapped out the trip on Google Earth, it had seemed so simple. Just a quick flight to Los Angeles, then one long flight over to Fiji, two short ones to Port Vila, and then on to Espiritu Santo. He had tabulated the flying time and estimated they would be flying for nineteen hours.

Between flights, he imagined hanging out in cool, foreign airports. As it turned out, the airports were definitely foreign, but they were not cool. They were sweltering and filled with people speaking languages he had never heard. And there were more than a few unpleasant odors. Hard plastic chairs kept him from resting comfortably, and the lack of Wi-Fi kept him from using his phone or laptop to access the web. He couldn't check email or Facebook or send travel updates as he had planned.

Now that the sun was setting, the clouds on either side of the plane were lit up with golden hues, but the ocean below was inky black. Caleb strained to see a light, a ship, an island—anything, really. But everything seemed to fade out of focus. He must have closed his eyes for just a moment, for suddenly the small plane shook back and forth violently, the engines raced, and the wheels thumped down hard on the runway.

Caleb looked up to see his father smiling at him. "We're here!" Dad announced. Out the window, Caleb saw a patch of thick, knee-high grass and a small terminal building with light shining out from all the cracks. Finally!

Why is it taking so long to get off the plane? Caleb wondered, feeling as if he couldn't stand being cooped up on the plane for even one more minute. Nobody else seemed in any great hurry, so all Caleb could do was wait.

Getting off the plane felt as if it took almost as long as the last leg of the trip. But finally, they were walking toward the terminal. What a relief it was to finally stretch his legs. Mostly, Caleb focused on his new surroundings.

"Look, Mom," Anna exclaimed excitedly a few seconds after they got inside. "There are the Williamses!"

Up ahead, Caleb saw Mr. and Mrs. Williams in the crowded terminal. After they all exchanged hugs, Caleb was anxious to get going. But Mr. Williams told them that they would need to wait for their luggage to be brought in from the plane.

"Tonight, we're going to feed you a quick supper and get you all off to bed," Mrs. Williams told Mom. "I know y'all must be exhausted from the trip."

The rest of the evening passed in a blur. The crowd jostled them as they collected their bags, and the hot evening air was filled with diesel fumes. They feasted on tasty sandwiches. Finally, after a cool shower, Caleb was able to stretch out on a real bed.

As he was drifting off to sleep, Caleb remembered something Mr. Williams had said to his dad as they were loading the luggage into the truck. "Jim, I know you have your heart set on preaching at evangelistic meetings along the west coast. But I could really use your help in Big Bay. We can talk more about it in the morning."

Big Bay, Caleb thought, curious but a little uneasy. *Where is Big Bay?*

ADJUSTMENTS

May 19

CALEB WOKE to bright tropical sunshine streaming through his window, and for a brief moment, he couldn't figure out where he was. Oh yeah, Vanuatu. Could it really be true? Wow! He could hear Mom and Dad talking in the small dining room just outside his door. Mentally he kicked himself. He had wanted to wake up early and be the first to see their new home in the daylight. Clearly, he had overslept. He picked his phone up off the bedside nightstand to check the time. Ten a.m.? How was that possible? What had he missed? Caleb hurried into the dining room, tugging his shirt over his head. "Sorry Dad, I didn't mean to sleep so late."

"So late?" Mom asked with a smile. "Son, it's five o'clock in the morning."

"What?" Caleb asked, confused. Dad held back a chuckle behind his coffee cup.

Caleb pulled out his phone again, "But my phone says ten a.m. How did it get off by five hours?"

This time Dad didn't try to conceal his laughter. "And what day does it say it is?" he asked.

Caleb glanced at his phone again. "It's Saturday, May 18."

Now Mom and Dad were both smiling, and Caleb was completely fuddled. "Son, it's ten a.m., Saturday, May 18, in Los Angeles. That was the last time your phone could automatically update the date and time. We crossed the date line as we flew. In Vanuatu, it's currently 5:05 a.m. on Sunday the 19th."

"Whoa," Caleb responded. "That's too weird. That means we're living in tomorrow."

Anna stumbled out of her bedroom. Her hair was frizzy, and she was rubbing her eyes. "Sorry I overslept," she mumbled. This time Caleb joined Mom and Dad in a chuckle. This was going to take a little getting used to.

"Dad and I couldn't sleep," Mom said. "We both woke up at two thirty, so we decided to go ahead and start our day. I'm glad you kids slept a little better."

Caleb heard a rather loud stomach gurgle, and he wasn't sure whether it came from his own stomach or Anna's. Either way, suddenly he was aware that he was hungry. Apparently Mom noticed it too. "There's some fresh fruit in the fridge and cereal and milk in the pantry," she said, pointing them in the right direction. "Get some breakfast, and join us."

"Milk in the pantry?" Anna asked. "Don't you mean in the fridge?"

"Nope," Dad answered. "And brace yourself. It tastes a bit different from the milk back home."

Caleb opened the pantry door and stared in amazement at boxes of milk in a line. For a moment, he thought it must be powdered milk, but a quick shake of a box revealed that it was full of liquid. *So this is missionary life*, Caleb thought. He hadn't even been awake ten minutes, and there were already too many weird things happening.

Caleb brought the milk and cereal to the table, while Anna rummaged through the cabinet and drawers to find bowls and spoons. He ate a few spoonfuls of cereal with the chalkiest tasting milk he had ever put in his mouth. Then he remembered what had been bothering him last night before he went to sleep.

"Dad, what was Mr. Williams talking to you about last night?" he asked. "We're going to the west coast, aren't we?"

"What?" Anna asked, turning sharply to look at Dad. Clearly, she hadn't heard them talking.

"I don't really know yet, son," Dad answered. "Last night is a bit of a blur. I guess this jet lag thing is pretty real when you cross this many time zones. I don't want to disturb the Williamses. When we hear them stirring, maybe we can get some answers." Dad gave his coffee a quick stir and set down the spoon before continuing. "While we're waiting, I want to remind you of Psalm 139:9–10: 'If I take the wings of the morning, and dwell in the uttermost parts of the sea; Even there shall thy hand lead me, and thy right hand shall hold me.'"

Dad paused again, letting the verse sink in to the weary traveler's heads. "We've come to the far side of the sea, but we can be sure that God will continue to lead us and protect us . . . even here."

"We all need to remember that we're here to serve God," Mom added. "The servant doesn't choose his tasks but follows the leading of the Master. You know that we've made plans before coming to Vanuatu, but whatever the next two months hold, we can count on God to lead us."

Caleb and Anna exchanged glances. He knew that they were both thinking about the mission station at Hakua. They both were looking forward to visiting the ruins of the old MacKenzie mission station. Surely, they would still get to go.

Caleb stared down into his cereal for a moment. He thought about their last Sunday at home. Mr. Smith had asked him to share with the youth group at church. Caleb had proudly made a brief presentation about the geography and people of Vanuatu.

He'd told them of his family's plans to travel up the west coast of Santo, holding evangelistic meetings in the major villages.

We have to go, he thought. *I already told everyone back home we were going.*

CHANGING PLANS

ANNA INTERRUPTED Caleb's brooding with an excited squeal. "Wow, look! A ship! It looks like it's just outside the front door!"

Everyone turned to look. A massive white ship glided through the glassy calm water of Segond Canal. Caleb grabbed his phone and shot out the door. He had to get a picture of this! He didn't bother pausing to put his shoes on but ran barefoot across the yard, leaned up against the main gate, and started snapping pictures as fast as he could. Anna and their parents soon joined him.

"Good morning!" Caleb heard a cheerful greeting from above and behind him. He turned to see Mr. and Mrs. Williams, both cradling mugs of coffee, standing on the balcony above the carport. "It's beautiful watching the ships go by in the morning." Mrs. Williams said. "Next time you'll have to watch from up here."

"Hope we didn't wake you." Mr. Williams said. "We were trying to let you rest. We know how tiring that trip is."

"When you feel like visiting, just come on up. The door's open," Mrs. Williams said so kindly that Caleb suddenly felt eager to take her up on her offer.

"We leave for church about nine," Mr. Williams said with a wave as he and his wife retreated into their apartment on the second floor of the mission house. The lower level consisted of a mission office and the guest apartment, where the Gristmans were staying.

After breakfast and showers, Caleb and Anna were itching to go upstairs. "Go," Mom said, laughing. "Just remember, this is their house. Don't just go barging in."

Caleb quickly led the way up the stairs and placed his hand on the doorknob. He stopped when Anna yanked on his arm. "Stop! Don't," she whispered forcefully. Her eyes pleaded with Caleb.

"She invited us," Caleb protested. "She said it was open."

"Mom said not to barge in!"

With a deep sigh, Caleb took his hand from the doorknob and knocked on the door. "It's Caleb and Anna," he announced, rolling his eyes at his little sister, who stuck her tongue out at him before releasing her breath in a sigh of relief.

"Come on in," they heard Mrs. Williams call. She was working at the counter at the front of the kitchen. Her silver-gray hair was piled up on top of her head, and an apron was pulled tight around her trim waist. She was leaning over the counter, briskly working a floury dough.

Anna's face lit up. "Can I help?"

"Sure, honey. Just grab yourself an apron there," Mrs. Williams answered, pointing to a drawer on the other side of the kitchen.

Caleb looked around the small kitchen. A large roasting pan held a fat hen with chunks of potato and pumpkin. Corn on the cob in bright green husks was piled on the countertop beside the stove. On the counter, a rolling pin lay beside a circle of dough. It looked like a wonderful meal was coming together, and that was something Caleb could always appreciate. However, making it didn't look like fun. He didn't understand Anna's excitement.

Caleb looked down at his phone. He really wanted to post an update on Facebook. "Mrs. Williams," he began, "Could I use your Wi-Fi?"

She smiled and pointed back downstairs. "Mr. Williams' office is the first door on the left. He'll get you set up."

"Thanks!" Caleb shouted, taking the stairs two at a time.

Just outside the door to Mr. Williams' office, the tile floor, cooled by a thin stream of air conditioning, felt cold under Caleb's bare feet. He raised his fist to knock on the door but paused when he heard Dad's voice.

"The kids really have their hearts set on trekking up the west coast. I think they'll be pretty disappointed if we don't."

"I understand," Mr. Williams answered. "But that's just not where I need you right now."

The rest of what Mr. Williams said was just a blur for Caleb as his thoughts raced. *So it's true. We came all this way, and we're not even going to get to see where Missionary MacKenzie lived.* Caleb gazed out the front door over the bright green trees and sparkling blue water without seeing a thing. His mind was far away in the youth class at First Community Church. He thought about how cool his plans had sounded when he shared them with his classmates. He remembered how proud he felt when Mr. Smith led the group in prayer and asked him to report on his mission trip when he returned. What would he say now? *This can't be happening.*

BEING

ANNA QUICKLY FOUND an apron and tied it around her waist. She wished Caleb hadn't left her alone quite so quickly in this new place with a woman she hadn't known very long. What if she said the wrong thing? What if she couldn't think of anything at all to say? "How can I help?" she asked Mrs. Williams, her voice sounding more confident than she felt.

"Thank you, honey," Mrs. Williams said cheerfully as she handed Anna a potato peeler and a bowl full of apples. "Would you peel these for me? I'm making an apple pie." Anna sat on one of the tall stools and began peeling while Mrs. Williams turned to work on the pie crust. "So, are you excited to be here in Vanuatu?" Mrs. Williams asked.

Anna thought for a minute before responding slowly: "I am, I think."

"You're not sure?" Mrs. Williams asked, turning to her.

Anna could feel Mrs. Williams' eyes on her, but she avoided making eye contact and focused on her peeling. "It's just . . . I'm not sure what I can do."

"What do you mean?" Mrs. Williams asked.

"Well," Anna said, the pace of her apple peeling slowing to match the speed of her words, "Dad plans on preaching evangelistic meetings. Mom brought supplies and plans to teach the church women how to make puppets. Caleb plans to map out the old MacKenzie mission station and post updates about our trip on the church Facebook page." She paused, stopping peeling altogether. "It just feels like everyone has something good to do but me. I'm not sure what *I'm* supposed to do."

"Hmm," Mrs. Williams answered thoughtfully. "I know how that feels. When I came to Vanuatu as a young mother, I was so busy taking care of my family and homeschooling my kids that it felt like I never did any real mission work." She smiled. "I remember visiting a church in Wisconsin, and the women wanted to know what I did on the mission field. I felt ashamed to tell them that I did the same thing on the mission field that I had been doing at home: I took care of my family."

Anna looked up in surprise. She had never thought about that. When Mr. and Mrs. Williams had come to First Community Church and talked about their mission work, Anna had just assumed they were both doing the work. "You mean you don't do any ministry?" she asked, ducking down to pick an apple peel off the floor.

"Over there, dear," Mrs. Williams smiled as she pointed out the trash can. "I guess that depends on what you call 'ministry.' I do help Mr. Williams now . . . far more than I ever did before. But along the way, God taught me some valuable lessons. He taught me that there is no higher calling than to be a wife and mother . . . to look after my family well and to teach my children to love him. But he also taught me that *being* is a lot more important than *doing*."

"What do you mean?" Anna asked.

Mrs. Williams took a deep breath and paused before answering. "Sometimes we get so focused on doing things for God, we forget that being the kind of Christian he wants us to be is a lot more important than any of the things we can do. In fact, I've learned that the most important thing in missions is being. God often uses our 'being' to bring others to faith in Christ." She placed her hands on Anna's, stopping her from peeling. When Anna looked up, she could see a look of determination in Mrs. Williams' eyes.

"Anna, I want you to do something for me."

Anna felt a surge of excitement and expectation as she waited for her assignment from Mrs. Williams. "In these next two months, don't focus on what you can do. Focus on being a godly young woman and a good friend to the girls you meet." She must have noticed Anna's letdown expression, because she added, firmly, "Trust me, Anna: who you are is more important than what you do."

Anna nodded weakly and bent to pick up another peel.

"Oh my goodness," Mrs. Williams said, turning back to her crust. "Time's getting away from us. We're going to have to hurry to get this finished in time. It's a good thing you're helping me!"

While she hurried to finish peeling the apples, Anna thought about what Mrs. Williams had said. Then, together, they put the finishing touches on two beautiful pies.

"Just in time," Mrs. Williams said as she popped the pies into the oven. "Thank you for helping me." Then, as she and Anna took off their aprons, she said, "You know, Anna, your *being* just might be the most important thing your family does on this trip."

Anna couldn't imagine that being true.

THE WHY

CHURCH WAS really something. In some ways, it was just like church at home. But in other ways, everything seemed totally new. Caleb couldn't understand how something could feel so familiar and so strange at the same time. And yet he loved it and was sad for the service to end.

After church, the Gristmans joined Mr. and Mrs. Williams on the balcony of the mission house for a fantastic meal of homemade chicken pot pie. The thatched roof of long, brown sago palm leaves blunted the force of the midday sun. A warm breeze blew across the ocean, driving endless lines of white-tipped waves toward the shore below. Mr. Williams was explaining to Dad the work needed to finish the mission clinic in Big Bay. Caleb half listened while he stuffed himself with pot pie.

It felt good to be full. But mixed with the good feeling was disappointment about where they would be spending the next two months. Caleb knew that Mom was right. They were here to serve God, and that meant doing whatever needed to be done. But he was struggling with the change of plans. He and Anna had dreamed of visiting the old MacKenzie house and the villages where Mr. and Mrs. MacKenzie had planted churches so long ago. He was willing to do whatever God wanted, but he really wanted to go the west coast.

During a pause in the conversation, Caleb asked, "Mr. Williams, I don't understand—why Big Bay instead of the west coast? Don't people on the west coast need Jesus just as much as the people in Big Bay?"

Mom looked uncomfortable, and even though he wasn't looking at Dad, Caleb was sure he was giving him a warning stare. But Mr. Williams smiled kindly. "That's a great question, Caleb. Let me ask you a question. Why do we do missions?"

"Because people need to believe in Jesus," Caleb quickly responded.

"Well, that's true," Mrs. Williams said. What do you think, Anna?"

Anna paused. She thought Caleb was right, but now she wasn't sure. "Um, because Jesus told us to?" She answered hesitantly.

"That's right as well," Mr. Williams answered. "Do you remember exactly what he told us to do?"

Caleb and Anna looked at one another. "Preach the gospel?" they answered together with a slight question in their voices. This conversation was getting complex.

"Actually," Mom spoke up, "it's a little more than that. Jesus told us, 'Go ye therefore, and teach all nations, baptizing them in the name of the Father, and of the Son, and of the Holy Ghost: Teaching them to observe all things whatsoever I have commanded you: and, lo, I am with you alway, even unto the end of the world. Amen.' Matthew 28:19–20. We do missions to fulfill the Great Commission."

"That's right!" Mr. Williams answered. "Missions is more than just telling people about Jesus. That could be better described as evangelism. Evangelism is telling people the good news in a way that will lead them to accepting Christ as their Savior. But the Great Commission gives us four key elements to missions. Can you tell me what they are?"

"Preaching," Caleb blurted out. "Preaching and baptizing."

"Okay, that's two—what do you think, Anna?"

Anna felt a little uncomfortable with the question. She thought before she spoke. "Teaching?" she asked.

"Good," Mr. Williams answered. "The four elements of missions we find in the Great Commission are going, preaching, baptizing, and teaching."

"But Jesus didn't actually say 'preaching,'" Dad chimed in.

"No, that's true." Mr. Williams answered. "He didn't in Matthew. However, in Luke 24:47, we read, 'Repentance and remission of sins should be preached in his name among all nations, beginning at Jerusalem.' So as missionaries, we understand that we are to both preach and teach the gospel."

"'Baptizing' tells us that we are to gather the new believers into communities of Christ followers—a local church. 'Teaching' tells us that we are to disciple the new believers by teaching them everything Jesus has taught us until, ultimately, they too will go and repeat the cycle."

None of this seemed to be answering his question, and Caleb's impatience was growing. "But I still don't understand why that means we should go to Big Bay instead of the west coast. We can preach, teach, and baptize the people there. Why change where we are going?"

"But that's exactly the point!" Mr. Williams said enthusiastically. "Why are you going where you're going? For that matter, why did you come to Vanuatu? You could have done those three things without leaving your home."

"B-b-because Jesus said to go?" Caleb stuttered. He was more than a little confused by Mr. Williams' question. Why had they spent so much time and money on travel? It was true, there were lots of unsaved people in their own hometown. Should they have stayed home?

"Jesus did tell us to go!" Mr. Williams exclaimed. "But where did he tell us to go?"

"To all nations," Dad answered. "That's the key. He told us to go to all nations, and the idea of 'all nations' is a recurring theme in the Bible. First, God told Abram, 'In thee shall all nations be blessed,' (Galatians 3:8). Then Jesus instructed us to go to 'all nations.'"

"Matthew 28:19!" Anna proudly shouted out the Bible reference she had learned so well before this trip.

"That's right," Dad smiled proudly at Anna, while Mom rubbed her back lovingly. "And finally, Revelation 5:9 tells us that Christ 'redeemed us to God by thy blood out of every kindred, and tongue, and people, and nation.' You see, Caleb, God's plan is for there to be a thriving church in every language in every nation."

"That's exactly right," Mr. Williams said. "And that's why I am asking you to change your plans. You see, the people on the west coast already know about Jesus. Do many of them still need to believe? Yes. But they have churches and pastors that are teaching them. The Tali who live in Big Bay are different."

Caleb was starting to feel a little guilty about being more concerned for his lost adventure than for the lost souls in Big Bay. "They've never heard?" he asked, increasingly resigned to their change of plans.

"While many of them have heard about Jesus, they still don't have a church," Mr. Williams explained. "We're starting a medical clinic so that a missionary and a pastor can live among them and teach them about Jesus until a strong local church is formed."

"Caleb," Mr. Williams said, leaning in and lowering his voice so everyone had to really listen to hear him. "You, Anna, and your parents are not just on an exciting adventure. You're a vital part of fulfilling God's plan for humanity."

Anna's eyes grew big, and a small gasp escaped her lips as Mr. Williams continued. "God will use your efforts here this summer to see that yet another tribe joins the celebration around his throne in eternity!"

Caleb sat back in his chair, stunned. He had never thought of it like that. Suddenly the coming months seemed a whole lot more important than seeing an old mission house or having great stories to tell when he returned home.

"Now, who wants some apple pie?" Mrs. Williams asked. "Anna helped me make it."

A SHOCKING DISCOVERY

May 27

CALEB WAS STARTING to question the wisdom of riding in the back of the truck. When they first pulled out of town on a nicely paved road, it seemed like a grand adventure. "Want to ride in the back?" Dad had asked. "Sure!" Caleb answered. It sounded like a great idea at the time. Cool tropical scenery, roadside ruins from World War 2, smooth road, wind blowing in your face . . . what could go wrong?

Today was moving day—time to begin their important mission to the Tali people by moving to their village to work on the mission clinic. Bright and early, Caleb had helped Dad and Mr. Williams pack the truck with suitcases, building supplies, and enough canned food to last the Gristman family a month.

But by far the most interesting cargo the truck would be carrying to Big Bay was Sam. Short and wiry with dark skin, Sam was fifteen, just one year older than Caleb. His tightly curled black hair was cropped close to his skull, and his clothes were tattered and torn. He was a student at the mission school in Luganville, one of the few Tali receiving an education. Mr. Williams thought it would be a great idea to take Sam home as a sort of bridge between the missionaries and his Tali kinsmen. When Mr. Williams had talked about the idea earlier, he had told Caleb that Sam was the nephew of a powerful Tali chief.

"This could be a divine appointment, Caleb," Mr. Williams had said earnestly. "Someone his own age just might be the witness Sam needs." He leaned in toward Caleb before continuing. "If Sam were to become a follower of Christ, he could have a powerful influence on the whole Tali tribe. Wouldn't it be wonderful if he were to become their first pastor?"

When everything was packed, the truck was so crowded that there was barely room for them all. Sam had climbed into the truck's bed and looked expectantly toward Caleb. For the last two hours, the truck had crawled over a brutal four-wheel-drive trail. Foaming low-water river crossings, hairpin turns up mountainsides, and dizzying drop-offs were all part of the road to Big Bay. Caleb found it hard to believe that trucks could even make it. Now he keenly felt each bump in the road.

While Caleb sat in the truck bed, trying hard to keep from bouncing out, Sam stood with his arms wrapped around the truck's roll bar. The truck paused on the road, and Sam motioned for him to stand. Caleb was only too happy to relieve the pressure on his aching tailbone. He gripped the truck's roll bar tightly with both hands and gingerly found footing among the suitcases and cartons of food. Before him, the mountains opened up into a massive V-shaped valley. Two rivers flowing from deep canyons joined in the valley far below. Sunlight glinted off the swift rapids. Gray stone riverbeds were bounded by lush jungle and stately coconut palm plantations.

"Joenriva," Sam said, pointing to the valley below. Caleb looked at him quizzically. "Joenriva" Sam repeated. "That is the village of Joenriva."

Suddenly Caleb understood: Yes, Joenriva. The place where two rivers—the Ora and the Lape—join together; the village where the Williamses were building the mission clinic. Caleb looked more closely and noticed a cluster of low thatched huts that spread out under the palm trees and down to the river's edge. On a low hill above the village stood the only metal-roofed house. Caleb knew it had to be the clinic building, his home for the next two months.

Caleb held tightly to the truck's roll bar as Mr. Williams began the curving descent into the valley below. The deeply rutted road often forced the truck to the very edge of sheer drop-offs. The tires frequently spun and spit gravel in a desperate bid to grip the roadbed. Caleb breathed a deep sigh of relief when they rounded the last bend and pulled to a stop in the village of Joenriva.

Caleb watched as Sam leaped from the truck and disappeared into the bushes. Mr. and Mrs. Williams, Mom, Dad, and Anna stepped out of the truck and stretched, talking excitedly about the road. A group of men walked down the center of the road to greet them. In the shadows of the trees, Caleb could see clusters of women and children. The Williamses continued talking, but one by one, the entire Gristman family fell into hushed silence.

Anna was the first to say it: "Mom! Dad! Everyone is naked!"

A NEW FRIEND

May 29

ANNA WAS DRYING the last of the breakfast dishes when she heard a faint voice on the front porch: "Misis?" Anna turned to look and spied a girl her age standing a few feet away from the door of the nurse's house. The girl was biting her finger and shifting her feet nervously. She shyly lifted her eyes toward the door and called out again, "Misis?"

"Mom," Anna called out. "I think she's looking for you." Anna joined her mother in answering the door, excited about the possibility of meeting a friend. The girl standing outside their door was shorter than Anna. Her thick black hair was braided tightly against her scalp, and she wore only a vine with a few leaves hanging from it, as was the custom of the women and girls in Joenriva.

"Hi!" Anna said brightly.

The girl ducked her head shyly and spoke softly. "Sori, Misis. Papa i senem mi blong mi mekem was."

Anna and her mom exchanged puzzled glances. Could the girl be speaking Bislama? Anna wondered. She had learned about this pidgin—a language used for communication between the 120 different language groups in Vanuatu. She knew that 40 percent of the words had English origins, so she strained her ear to pick out words she could understand.

"Bae mi was," the girl said. Catching the confused look on Anna's face, she pantomimed a scrubbing motion. "Bae mi wasem klos."

"Klos?" Mom repeated.

"Io, bae mi wasem klos," the girl replied. Then she reached out and rubbed the fabric of Anna's skirt between her fingers. "Klos," she repeated, tugging at Anna's skirt.

"Mom, I think she wants to wash our clothes!" Anna exclaimed.

"Yes," the girl's face lit up with a smile. "Bae mi wasem klos!"

"I'm not sure," Mrs. Gristman said hesitantly.

But now the barrier was broken. All the shyness seemed to evaporate from the girl, and she smiled enthusiastically. "Nem blong mi Mari," she said, pointing toward her chest. "Nem blong yu?" She pointed at Anna.

"Name belong you . . . name! She wants to know our names!" Anna squealed, excited to be communicating. "My name is Anna," she told Mari with a big smile.

Mari took hold of her arm and smiled at Mrs. Gristman. "Mi, Anna, go was nao! Yes?" Mrs. Gristman stalled, "Oh, we can wash our own clothes. But thank you. Thank you very much!"

Mari bobbed her head with a big smile, clearly not understanding Mrs. Gristman at all. "Gud gud, Mi, Anna go was nao. Warem klos?"

"Oh, please Mom, please!" Anna begged.

"Well, I never!" exclaimed Mrs. Gristman. Quick as a flash, Mari was through the door of the nurse's house and was gathering dirty clothes and used linens. Each time she picked up more, she beamed a huge smile at Anna and Mrs. Gristman, bobbed her head enthusiastically, and said, "Mi, Anna go was nao? Yes!"

Mrs. Gristman turned to Anna. "I guess we are going to wash clothes! Yes!"

"Yes!" Mari and Anna echoed.

Once Anna and Mari had gathered up all the dirty clothes, Mari led Mrs. Gristman and Anna down the narrow dirt road toward the river. For the two nights since their arrival, Anna had been hearing the roar of the river over the rapids, but she had yet to see or visit the river. The view past the curve in the road made Anna draw in her breath sharply. Before her, two silver ribbons joined together to form a braided river. The morning sun sparkled off the water until it hurt her eyes. On the green-cloaked mountainside beyond the river, a wispy white waterfall tumbled into the valley.

"Oh, Mom," Anna cried. "It's so pretty!"

Mari led Anna and Mrs. Gristman down the path where a clear stream of spring water bubbled up and joined the river. She dumped the clothes on the black sand and, with a big smile, pointed to some smooth stones. "Yumi was!"

Once they had finished washing their clothes, Mari had coaxed Anna into the river for a quick swim. The water, although swift, wasn't deep, and Anna felt perfectly safe. Afterward, Anna sat with her feet in the cold water and looked out at the scene before her. Up and down the river, women were gathered, scrubbing cooking dishes. Naked children ran screaming along the riverbank and plunged into pools of calm water below the rapids.

"Thank you, Jesus," she prayed. "Thank you for bringing me to such an amazing place. Thank you for bringing Mari to be my friend. Help me to share your love with her."

UPRIVER

June 10

CALEB LOOKED AROUND the table in the early morning light. Mom and Dad were sipping cups of instant coffee, and he and Anna both had cups of instant hot chocolate. They had just finished a breakfast of eggless pancakes and homemade syrup. Mom and Anna were both wearing sweatshirts. They had all learned a lot over the last two weeks. Mom had learned to cook meals without any fresh ingredients. They had all learned to overlook the nakedness of the villagers. Much to their surprise, they had all learned that mornings can be quite cool in the tropics.

Together, they finished their family devotions. They prayed for Grandpa and Granny Gristman so far away in America, for Mr. and Mrs. Williams in Luganville, and for the Tali villagers all around them. Each morning, they prayed for Sam—that Caleb would be a witness to him. Caleb was still recovering from the shock of seeing Sam emerge from the bushes in only a loin cloth shortly after he had returned home.

In Luganville it had been easy to assume that Sam was just like him, only—given the tattered state of his clothes—a little poorer. After all, he knew that most Ni-Vanuatu were poor subsistence farmers barely producing enough to feed themselves. He had been amazed to learn that only 14 percent of the people had other jobs, and those who did typically only earned 25,000 vatu—or $219 dollars—per month. Seeing Sam's sudden transformation once they returned to Tali territory made it abundantly clear to Caleb that Sam wasn't just poor. Sam required more than the education he was receiving at the mission school. He needed to go beyond knowing about Jesus to truly knowing him.

Caleb thought about the devotion Dad had just shared from Romans 8:28: "We know that all things work together for good to them that love God, to them who are the called according to his purpose." Sitting here in a remote mission outpost, Caleb understood the words in a way he never had before.

Because the income from Dad's ministry as an evangelist had never quite been enough to cover the family's needs, Dad also served as the maintenance man for First Community Church and worked as a handyman around the community.

"You know, Dad, I've always seen your handyman work as an unfortunate necessity, or maybe even part of your suffering for Christ," Caleb mused. "I never realized that it could be fulfilling a greater purpose. It's because of the things you've learned to do as a handyman that we can be a part of reaching the Tali for Christ."

"You're right, son," Mom replied. "When your dad first quit his job to begin his ministry as an evangelist, I struggled with the lack of money. I remember many times asking God to provide so that your father wouldn't have to take odd jobs to make ends meet. But it's true—all things *do* work together for good for those called according to God's purpose. Because of those odd jobs, your dad has the knowledge and skill to finish this mission clinic.

"Preach it," Anna shouted in a deep voice that sounded a lot like Mr. Tialdo on the front pew when the pastor back home "got anointed." That brought a good-natured laugh from everyone.

But Mom wasn't finished. "I think the most exciting part is realizing that God will use what you and Anna are learning now for his purposes in the future!"

"Speaking of skills," Dad said, "Caleb, why don't you use your technology skills to send out an update." They had purchased a router that had been advertised as working worldwide. But much to their disappointment, they had found that it didn't receive any signal in the deep river valley.

"Mr. Williams told me that if you hike up the Ora about an hour, there's a hilltop where you can get reception. Sam can show you. How about the two of you hike up there today and see if you can make a Facebook post so our church and family will know how we're doing?"

"Awesome!" Caleb shouted. "I'll go get Sam."

An hour later, Sam and Caleb stood on the banks of the Ora River. The clear, cold water rippled and gurgled over the large stones that made up the riverbed. Thick mats of green moss covered the rocks at the water's edge. The banks of the river were made up of a tangled maze of gray stones that varied in size from a softball to a Volkswagen Beetle.

Caleb slung the strap of a small waterproof case over his shoulder. Inside was the satellite internet router and his phone. Sam carried a small basket made of tightly woven cream-colored pandanas leaves. Sam pulled the top open and motioned for Caleb to look. Caleb glanced inside to see several freshly baked taro tubers.

Sam smiled. "Lunch!" he said. Caleb's stomach turned at the thought of eating the local staple. He just smiled back at Sam. *One hour up, and one hour down,* he thought. *We should be back long before lunch.*

Sam led, deftly leaping from boulder to boulder. Caleb raced after him. This was more like it. It wasn't that Caleb didn't like helping his dad. He did. It was just that painting and installing plumbing got . . . well, boring. This was more like the adventure he had envisioned when they had first planned to come to Vanuatu.

Caleb gasped in awe as they rounded the first bend on the Ora. The steep mountainsides pressed right up to the river. Up ahead, the open valley narrowed into a slot canyon. The sheer gray stone of the canyon soared hundreds of feet above the river. Far overhead, the two stone faces nearly touched. Shafts of golden sunshine shot through the jungle canopy growing on each clifftop.

"Wow!" Caleb shouted. "This is awesome!"

Sam turned and grinned. "Just wait till you see the waterfalls. I'll race you to the first one!" Sam sprinted up the riverbed. Caleb struggled after him, feeling the waterproof case thump into his back with each stride. Every time Caleb took his eyes off his feet, he stumbled over a stone. In spite of his sandals, he still managed to stub his toes. In front of him,

Sam ran barefoot with his loincloth streaming out behind him. It seemed as if his feet barely touched the stones. How did Sam run that fast without breaking his leg?

TORN BETWEEN WORLDS

AFTER CALEB HAD LEFT WITH SAM to go upstream, Anna and Mari headed to the river to wash the clothes. It had taken a few trips to the river before Mom felt comfortable letting Anna and Mari go alone. Anna glanced over at Mari. Even though they had known each other for only two weeks and struggled to communicate, Mari was her friend.

Mari caught her eye, and they shared a smile. "Yumi was, mo afta, yumi plei lelui," Mari said with a smile, bobbing her head up and down with her words to try to help Anna understand.

Lelui, Anna had learned, was a game of chase. In the evenings, the children ran screaming with laughter between the palm trees and across the open spaces in the village, with cries of "Yu lelui! Yu lelui" echoing through the village. It took only a few minutes that first evening for Anna to realize that "yu lelui" meant "you're it!"

Anna looked around the village. Pigs grunted happily as they rooted beside bamboo huts. A ragged-looking rooster chased a squawking hen across the

road in front of them. Smoke from cooking fires rose through the thatched roofs of kitchens. Naked young children with runny noses played in the dusty yards in front of the kitchens. An old man wearing only a loin cloth used an axe to split firewood.

A month ago, Anna never would have believed a place like Joenriva existed. In fact, she felt as if she were living in another world. She wished she could share this world with Sarah, her best friend back home. Far away, Sarah was getting ready for church—putting on her Sunday dress and best shoes. Her family would drive down a smooth, paved road to the church, park between brightly painted yellow lines on a concrete parking lot, and walk up clean sidewalks through neatly maintained lawns. Sarah wouldn't get her dress dirty today, and her feet wouldn't touch the mud.

Anna looked down at her dress, already worn and faded from being washed on stones and dried in the sun. Mud squeezed up between her toes as she walked the muddy footpath beside the rutted dirt road. Within a week of being at Joenriva, Anna had stopped wearing shoes. For a minute, Anna felt torn between the kind of girl that loved a place like Joenriva and the kind of girl that dressed up in Sunday dresses in America. What would Sarah think of her now? What would she think of Mari?

Anna looked at Mari and tried to imagine her through Sarah's eyes. Her arms were full of the Gristmans' dirty laundry, but Mari wore only the *lif nangari*, a thin vine tied around her waist with three long, slim leaves hanging in the front and three hanging in the back. Thick scars marked her belly where her father had cut her to bleed out the "bad blood" when she had been sick as a toddler. Deep open sores covered with flies pitted her legs.

Suddenly, Anna felt an ache in her heart. Hot tears welled up in her eyes, and it became hard to swallow. What a difference it would make in Mari's life once the clinic was finished. Medicine would be available for her sores, and no more children in Joenriva would have to get those ugly cuts on their stomachs. A whispered prayer sprang from Anna's heart: "Jesus, help Daddy to finish the clinic. Help Mr. and Mrs. Williams to find the right nurse to work here. Help me. Help me to be a true friend to Mari and show her your love."

STORM CLOUDS

FRUSTRATED, CALEB gave up running and kept his eyes on the stones in front of him, carefully taking one step at a time. Back at the mission house, Mr. Williams had told him that the rivers were the highways of the interior. Caleb had imagined running up grassy riverbanks. Instead, the uneven riverbed forced him to slow down and choose each step with care. Caleb was so focused on his footing that he nearly bumped into Sam.

"Look at that," Sam said, pointing up.

High above, a stream of water gushed from a slit in the cliff face. It crashed into a pool at the base of the cliff before pouring into the main flow of the river. Caleb stood transfixed. It was like nothing he had ever seen.

"The best part is the shrimp," Sam told him.

"Shrimp?" Caleb asked. "In a river?"

"Yes! The stream above the waterfall is filled with thousands of amazing shrimp. Once you climb up there, you can scoop them up."

Caleb didn't know which he found more amazing—that there were shrimp in a river, or that Sam had climbed to the top. How cool would it be to take some shrimp home to Mom and Dad? After two weeks of canned food . . . fresh shrimp for dinner! Caleb's mouth watered just thinking about it.

Sam flashed a huge grin, as if he could read Caleb's thoughts. "Come on," he said. "I can show you how to climb it. I'm sure you will get phone reception at the top."

Just beyond the waterfall, Sam showed Caleb a series of grooves cut into the rock. "Here, follow me. Watch carefully where I put my feet and hands."

Step by step, Caleb followed Sam up the cliff face. Two thirds of the way up, his legs began to tremble, and the pack on his back began to feel heavy. Finally, he saw Sam reach the top and lean back over the edge to extend a hand. Breathing heavily, Caleb scrambled over the top of the cliff and sat down, trembling, quite sure he had never done anything so hard in his life.

Beside him, the smooth stream of water leaped over the lip of a small pool before plunging dizzily to the floor of the canyon below. Caleb heard a splash and looked over his shoulder to see Sam swimming in the round pool above the waterfall. Above the first pool were three others separated by small waterfalls. Caleb watched as Sam scampered over the waterfall at the top of the pool. He stopped for just a moment before diving into the second pool.

"Come on," Sam yelled.

Carefully, Caleb backed away from the edge of the cliff and looked at the series of waterfalls and pools. Each round pool was surrounded by short grass and neat bushes. It was beautiful, like a well-tended garden. Caleb laid his pack on the ground,

took off his shoes, and cautiously edged into the first pool. Sam joined him, and they floated over to the slot in the stone where the stream leaped from the cliff face into a long waterfall.

Sam held his hand in the stream just before it flowed through the slot. He sat perfectly still, concentrating deeply, with a look of anticipation on his face. Suddenly, the muscles in his arm twisted, and he lifted his hand high in the air. In his grip was the largest shrimp Caleb had ever seen. Sam beamed. "You go set up your phone. I will catch our dinner!"

Caleb climbed out of the pool and shook himself dry as best he could. He found a large, flat rock above the pool and carefully opened his waterproof case. Sure enough, as soon as the satellite router powered up, it gave off a faint ping, indicating that it had a signal. Next, on his phone, Caleb sent the emails to Granny and Grandpa that he and Anna had been writing each day. Finally, he logged on to Facebook, went to the First Community Church page, and posted a quick status update, letting their church family know that they were all safe and well.

While he waited for the incoming emails to download, Caleb sat back and watched Sam catching shrimp. He was slowly circling the pool, reaching into nooks and crannies between the stones. Each time he pulled out a fat shrimp, he smiled triumphantly at Caleb and stuffed it into his pandanas bag. Caleb wondered if he had taken the taro out first or if the tubers were getting all slimy. He was about to go see how many shrimp Sam had caught when he heard the chime of a Facebook message.

"Hi Caleb, Mr. Smith here. Just wanted you to know that the class is praying for you. Trust your trip up the west coast is going well. Can't wait to hear your stories."

Wow! Caleb thought. *Here I am, all the way on the other side of the world, and we can have instant communication. How cool is that?*

"Thanks so much for the prayers," Caleb wrote back. "We never made it to the west coast. Turns out God had different plans. We're helping the Williamses finish a medical clinic for the Tali tribe. But you'll never believe where I am right now! I'm sitting at the top of a waterfall in the middle of the jungle, while Sam, my Tali friend, is catching shrimp!"

"Wow! Sounds amazing," Mr. Smith's answer came in just a few minutes. "I know that sometimes things don't work out the way we planned them. Just remember, 'All things work together for good to them that love God, to them who are the called according to his purpose.'"

"LOL, that was the passage Dad read today during our family devotions. I think God must be trying to get a message through to me! BTW, when the class prays, please pray for my Tali friend, Sam. He's a great guy, but he really needs the Lord."

"Will do. I'm headed to the church right now. We'll pray especially for Sam today. We are praying for you and your family as well. Let me know if there's anything else we can pray about."

Caleb had forgotten that it was Sunday in America. It seemed so strange that today was Monday in Vanuatu but Sunday there. Caleb thought about his friends getting ready for church. Soon they would be driving down paved highways and walking into a clean, carpeted, air-conditioned church building. Meanwhile, he was here with Sam at the top of a waterfall in the middle of the jungle. It seemed hard to believe it was even the same world. Yet he wouldn't trade places with his friends for anything.

Caleb started to reply, but he heard the triple beep, beep, beep that signaled that the satellite router had lost its connection. He looked up at the sky in confusion and saw dark, heavy thunderclouds blotting out the horizon.

"Hey, Sam," Caleb called out, pointing toward the clouds.

Sam held up a basket bulging with squirming shrimp. "Pack up, and let's go," Sam said.

SWEPT AWAY!

AFTER ANNA AND MARI finished the day's washing, they started a game of *lelui* (chase). This time, instead of running between palm trees and thatched huts as they normally did each evening, they dashed between the braided streams of the Jordan River. How different this river was from the ones Anna had known in America. Instead of a deep stream flowing between two banks, the Jordan spread out over a wide expanse of riverbed. It broke into dozens of small streams that meandered between beaches of black sand and banks of round gray stones before joining and then separating again. Anna was intrigued by the black sand. No wonder they called this region of the Western Pacific "Melanesia"—the Black Islands.

When Anna chased after Mari, she tried to stick to the stretches of black sand, but Mari always dashed away over the stones before diving into the next pool. Anna winced as she tried to run across the river stones. How could Mari run over them so fast?

Soon other children picked up the cry of "lelui," and it seemed that half of the village children joined their game. They sprinted along the narrow beaches of sand and stone, splashing through shallow pools. Everyone was having so much fun! Anna tried to keep up, but she fell far behind. Her feet were too tender to run at full speed over the rough stones. She waded out into a pool and let the cool water caress her sore feet. She felt left out as she watched Mari and the other children at a distance.

Watching the game of chase play out far down the riverbed, Anna was surprised by a shout. Only moments ago, one of the village women had been squatting beside the river, using the coarse sand to wash out a cooking pot. Now she was standing and screaming angrily at the children in the Tali language. Soon several other women joined her, yelling at the children and making swooping motions up and down the river. One grabbed a small boy who was playing in the sand beside her and began dragging him up the riverbank, screaming in a shrill voice all the while.

Why were they angry, Anna wondered. Was it something she had done? For the first time since coming to Joenriva, Anna felt scared. She was surprised by the harsh tone of the women and confused by their wild gestures. What had she done wrong? Was it because she had started a game of *lelui* in the middle of the day? Was there a rule about *lelui* that she didn't know? She looked back over the path she had followed. Had she disturbed someone's washing laid out to dry on the black stones?

Something wet and slimy slithered past Anna's foot. She looked down, screamed, and jumped back. The pool she had been standing in was gone, and a large brown eel, looking just like a snake, whipped its way past her and across the wet pebbles at Anna's feet. Suddenly, Mari was beside her again. She threw a large stone at the eel's head, stunning it and causing it to writhe in pain.

Quickly, Mari snatched up the eel. "Bae yumi kakai! Namari hemi swit gud!"

Anna had no idea what Mari was saying. Across the riverbed, the water had stopped flowing, and the pools had disappeared. Only a few shallow pools remained. Children ran from puddle to puddle, scooping up fish and eels. Where had the water gone?

The strident screaming of the women pulled Anna's attention back to the village. The younger mothers were clutching their babies, standing on the low hill just beyond the riverbank. Some were starting to weep. A child screamed, and Anna turned back to see an older woman holding a long branch. She was running up the riverbed and whipping the children, herding them toward shore. What was happening?

Mari was still clutching the squirming eel in one hand. With the other, she grabbed Anna's hand and quickly pulled her across the riverbed. Together they scrambled up the clay bank that separated the village of Joenriva from the riverbed. Mari, panting from running so hard, simply said, "Graon I brok."

Anna had no idea what she meant. How she wished she could understand.

Once atop the bank, they stood in a crowd of women who were screaming at the children still picking up the flopping fish. All but one boy fled the riverbed. He stubbornly refused to listen to the women and scrambled from one shrinking pool to the next, gathering more and more fish, moving farther and farther away from the bank.

Anna heard a roaring noise. She gasped in surprise to see a massive collection of boulders and stones shooting out of the canyon upstream. Angry, reddish-brown water swept them rapidly down-stream. Suddenly, Anna understood the shouting of the women. They were warning the children! Too late, the young boy heard the roar of the stones. He turned and ran for the riverbank. His mother, screaming in grief, tried to race toward him, but the other women held her back.

Anna couldn't watch. The screams and sobs of grief around her were enough to tell her that the boy hadn't made it to safety. She suddenly felt sick all the way through. The river had transformed from a kind friend to a scary and dangerous force. The boy's mother collapsed on the riverbank, wailing in grief. The other women cried out with her, with long tragic wails of "O wei! O wei!"

Drawn by the noise, Mom ran down to the riverbank. She took Anna in her arms and held her tightly. They both stared at the raging torrent below and the grieving women around them. Suddenly, Anna had a terrible thought: *Caleb!* "Mama, what about Caleb?" she asked, her voice trembling. "Is he okay?"

Caleb had hiked up that river! Where was he? What had happened to him? Had he been caught in that angry swirl of stone and water?

A GOOD FRIEND

CALEB REPACKED the router and phone as quickly as he could. Then, following Sam's lead, he lay flat on his belly and slowly squirmed off the cliff face until his feet caught on the first toeholds below. Going down was an entirely different experience than going up. Each time Caleb looked down to find the next toehold, his head swam. He was thankful that Sam was just below him and able to guide his feet the few times he missed the notches cut into the stone. Just as his feet came to a rest on the solid floor of the canyon, the heavens opened, and a torrential rain poured down.

If coming upstream on the uneven stones had been hard, going downstream when his arms and legs were trembling from the exertion of climbing down the cliff face was almost impossible. Rain pelted him, soaking him to the bone. Caleb's legs felt wooden. Each step required a huge effort. He no longer tried to look at the scenery around him, although he knew it was amazing. No, all he was focused on now was the next step and getting home.

Caleb was wading through a pool of waist-deep water when, suddenly, the water dropped to his knees and then his ankles. Caleb stopped and stared dumbly at a large fish flopping in a shallow pool. One part of his brain told him that something was wrong—that a fish that size shouldn't be in such a shallow pool. But the rest of him was just relieved that the water was shallower here and not as difficult to walk through. Caleb felt his arm being yanked sharply, and he looked up in stunned surprise.

"Caleb! Run!" Sam shouted.

Caleb stared at Sam. What was wrong? But Sam didn't take time to explain. Instead, he grabbed Caleb's wrist and dragged him, running and stumbling, over the river stones lining the narrow canyon. Caleb's feet slipped on the mossy rocks. Twice he fell, banging his shins sharply on the river stones, but Sam forcefully pulled him to his feet again and urged him on. Caleb's heart was pounding now. The river, rushing by just a few minutes before, had slowed to a trickle. Where had the water gone? Why was Sam in such a hurry?

Ahead, the gray stone walls of the canyon spread apart slightly. A house-sized boulder sat at the base of the cliff on the eastern side of the canyon. Beyond it, the ground sloped up to the cliff. Sam scrambled up the side of the boulder.

"Quick!" he said. "Grab my hand."

Caleb struggled to follow Sam up the rough side of the stone. Once they reached the top of the boulder, Sam urged Caleb on further. Together, they rushed up the sloping ground. To Caleb's surprise, a rough ladder had been cut into the stone wall above them.

"Come on!" Sam urged!

Caleb had just begun to climb the rough stone ladder when he heard a terrific roar behind him. He turned to look. Hundreds of boulders and thousands of smaller stones were bouncing and skipping down the riverbed between the narrow canyon walls, crashing off the cliff faces and each other.

"Jesus! Help us!" Caleb cried out.

Suddenly, he felt a large hand grab the back of his shirt and the strap on his pack. He felt himself spinning . . . flying through the air. He landed with a thud on the floor of a small cave.

Caleb sat up and looked into the canyon below. An angry brown stream of muddy water mixed with stone roared through the crevasse. The riverbed, and even the large boulder they had climbed, were buried beneath its angry waves.

Caleb looked around the small cave. Sam was picking himself up off the floor. Between them was a short, stout man. His hands and feet were square and thickly callused. He wore a tattered pair of shorts and a torn T-shirt, and he was chuckling.

"O' mi ting se bae yufala I lus ia! Mi stap wajem yufala, mi ting se, no be tufala i neva save win ia! No!

No!" The old man rocked back and forth and punctuated his words with laughter.

Dazed and confused, Caleb looked at Sam. "What just happened?" he asked. "Who is this?"

Sam and the old man engaged in a rapid-fire exchange in the Tali language. The old man continued to rock back and forth, shaking his head and chuckling the whole time. Finally, Sam turned to Caleb. "Sometimes in heavy rains there is a landslide in the mountains that blocks the river. That's why the river stopped flowing. The landslide formed a dam that held back the river. But these dams never last long. I knew that soon the dam would burst and create a flash flood. When the dam breaks, the water rushes through the canyon so rapidly that it scatters stones and boulders in front of it. If we had been caught on the floor of the canyon when the flash flood struck, we would have been killed."

Caleb sat back, stunned. "That's why you grabbed me and dragged me up here!" He exclaimed.

"That's right," Sam replied. "Only we never would have made it if Olfala Joe hadn't helped us. When the rain started, he took shelter in the cave. He saw us coming and was able to pull us up into the cave once we got close."

"O mi ting se bae mi no save mekem," Olfala Joe chuckled. "Mi no ting se mi gat naf paoa blong pulum tu bigfala boe olsem yutufala blong yu kam antap! Be, taem mi harem yangfala ia i krae aot long Jisas, wan taem nomo, mi bin harem se mi mi gat naf paoa blong mekem!"

Caleb looked at Sam for a translation. Sam seemed to hesitate. "Olfala Joe is a Christian. He was the first Tali to believe on Jesus. He said he was afraid he wouldn't be able to lift us to safety. But when you cried out to Jesus, he suddenly had the power he needed to pull us up into the cave."

"No, yu luk. Emi no Olfala Joe we i bin sevem yu! No Gat!" Joe shook his head and continued chuckling. "Hem i Jisas, we I bin harem krae blong yu mo i bin sevem yutufala!"

Sam continued. "He says, it wasn't him that saved us. It was Jesus." Sam's faced twisted a bit, and Caleb realized he was struggling in his heart. He realized that his class at church was probably praying for Sam right now.

"Sam, you're a good friend," Caleb said solemnly. "You could have left me in the river and saved yourself, but you didn't. You risked your life to save mine from the flash flood. Jesus is a good friend too. He didn't have to die, but he did so that he could save me and Olfala Joe . . . and you too."

Sam bit his lip and looked out over the flooded river. Caleb wanted to continue, but Olfala Joe put his hand on his arm to stop him. Instead, they all sat together silently and watched the river roar past.

After a while, Sam cleared his throat and wiped his eyes. He looked at Caleb as he reached into his bag full of shrimp. "We're gonna be here a while. Want some taro?"

THE LONG NIGHT

IN MOMENTS, it seemed as if the entire village had joined Anna and her mother on the riverbank. The women joined in the wailing, but the men began shouting loudly in Tali. Dad ran to the bank to see what was causing the commotion. One of the men who spoke a bit of English explained: "Landslides in the mountains create temporary dams on the river. When the dam breaks, a flash flood follows. A boy was in the river when the flood came. We need to search downstream to see if we can find him. If he's still alive, he'll need a doctor."

Dad ran back to the clinic to grab a rope. Mom and Anna slowly followed. Tears welled up in Anna's eyes and spilled down her cheeks. The wailing of the women caused knots in her stomach and a lump in her throat. "Oh, Mama, what if he's dead? What if the stones killed him? And, and," she stuttered, "what about Caleb? Oh, Mama! What if something happened to Caleb?"

Mom pulled Anna close as Anna began to sob. "Anna, in times like this, we pray. Jesus can help that boy. He can take care of Caleb. Rather than fearing what might have happened, let's ask Jesus for help."

Anna squeezed her mother even tighter, and together they began to pray. Sometimes Anna found the words catching in her throat—they couldn't get past that awful lump. But Mom continued to pray in a low, quiet voice. Slowly, Anna's sobs subsided, and she began to feel peace.

"Anna, look." Anna looked up at her mother and was surprised to see tears staining her cheeks as well. But then she noticed that her mother was looking off to her left. Anna followed her gaze and saw Mari standing there with tears streaming down her face.

Anna left her mother's arms and went and gave Mari a big hug. She felt Mari shaking as she sobbed. Suddenly, Anna understood: Mari didn't know how to pray. She didn't know the peace that Jesus could give. Anna started crying all over again—not in fear or grief, but because she felt sorry for Mari. If only she knew the right words to tell her.

In a flash, Anna knew what she needed to do. No, she didn't know the Tali words to tell Mari about Jesus, but she could pray. Holding Mari tightly, she started to pray, just as her mother had prayed with her. "Jesus, we need your help. Would you save this little boy? Would you help the men find him and bring him back safely? And Jesus, please protect Caleb. Oh, Jesus, please bring him back to us safely."

As Anna prayed, she felt Mari begin to take deeper breaths. Stepping back, Anna looked into Mari's face. This time, Anna saw hope. "Jisas?" Mari said softly. "Jisas bae i givhan?"

Mom led Anna and Mari onto the porch of the clinic building. She went inside and brought out cups of hot tea and some of the cookies they had brought with them from town. The three of them sat quietly on the porch, slowly drinking their tea, nibbling on the dry cookies, and waiting for news.

The sun was starting to set when they heard a loud cry downstream. Mari listened intently. "Oli faenem!" She cried. "Oli faenem!" Quick as a flash, she darted off the porch and ran into the village. Anna desperately wanted to follow, but Mom warned her off with a stern look. Together, they waited until a group of men emerged from the village. Daddy was in the lead, and between them, they carried the limp body of a small boy.

They carried him into the nearly completed clinic building, and Daddy, covered with mud, took Mom into his arms. "He's alive," he said. "He really needs a doctor, but unfortunately, we're all he has."

Now it was Mom's turn to sob. She buried her face in Daddy's shoulder and shook with deep sobs.

"Amy, I'm so sorry I sent him upstream today. I had no idea . . ." Daddy's voice broke for a second, and then he continued. "We have to trust God. Right now, we can't do anything for Caleb, but we can help this boy. Come with me. I need your help."

Mom and Dad started into the clinic. Anna wanted to follow, but Mom shook her head firmly. "Not now, Anna." So Anna waited alone on the porch. Waited, prayed, and worried all alone in the gathering darkness.

GIANTS IN THE NIGHT

CALEB LOOKED at the taro Sam was offering. He didn't like taro when it was hot, much less when it was cold, and even less when it had been stuffed in a bag with wiggly shrimp. He shook his head. "That's okay, I'm not hungry." He said, feeling guilty. He was starving. It had been the hardest day of his life. He was wet, cold, tired, and desperately hungry.

Olfala Joe pulled a few sticks and a piece of wood from his basket. Arranging them on the floor, he sang a song to himself and worked one of the sticks back and forth over the piece of wood. Soon a tendril of smoke rose from the wood. Olfala Joe bowed low over the wood and blew. Moments later, a small flame flickered in the growing darkness of the cave.

Sam moved farther back into the cave and began to pull dried sticks from a hole in the wall. He handed them to Olfala Joe, who gently pushed three of the sticks together until their ends met in the tiny flame. Slowly, the fire grew, catching hold of the sticks. Olfala Joe reached into Sam's basket, drew out three taro, and laid them between the sticks to warm by the flame.

Caleb looked out at the torrent below. "When will it go down?" he asked.

Sam shrugged. "It depends on the rain. If it quits raining, then we will be able to walk home in the morning. If it keeps raining . . ." He let his words trail off.

Caleb thought he would never be able to sleep, but the next thing he knew, Olfala Joe was shaking him awake. It was dark except for the soft glow of the firelight. Olfala Joe smiled and handed him a steaming hot piece of taro and a handful of roasted shrimp. "Kakae, kakae, Yu no wori, bae yumi prae. God i save mekem ren i finis."

After they finished off the shrimp and taro, Caleb did his best to find a smooth portion of the cave wall to lean against. Olfala Joe pulled a pan flute out of his bag and began to play a simple repeating melody. Caleb stared into the flames, which he could have sworn were dancing to the music.

Sam interrupted his thoughts. "Before, giants lived here in this cave. Two brothers, with no wife." Caleb looked at him, wondering if this was a tall tale. Sam could see the skepticism on his face. "It's true," he

insisted. "Two giants lived here. They were the ones who rolled that boulder to the bottom of the cliff and piled dirt on top. Then they cut a ladder into the stone."

Caleb didn't know what to think. He didn't believe any two men would be able to roll that massive boulder. "What happened to them?" he asked.

Sam motioned to Olfala Joe. "Him. Him and his brothers happened to them. They caught them one day in the river and surprised them. The giant brothers tried to run back to their cave, but they shot them with arrows till they died."

Caleb looked at Olfala Joe, then back at Sam. He couldn't decide if he believed the story.

Exhaustion overcame Caleb, and he slept. All night, he had strange dreams of giants rolling stones down the riverbed and of short, stocky men shooting him with arrows. Whenever he stirred, the small fire still flickered in the cave, and soft tones of Olfala Joe's pan flute washed over him.

Caleb awoke to bright sunlight shining in his eyes and the soft sounds of birds singing. He groaned as he sat up. He felt sore all over. Looking around, he noticed that the fire had died, and Olfala Joe and Sam were both gone.

Gingerly, Caleb made his way over to the mouth of the cave. The river, raging and angry red the night before, had retreated and was once again a smooth, clear stream dancing along its pebble-strewn bed. Olfala Joe and Sam were picking up pieces of wood that had been washed down from the mountains in the flood. Sam stopped and waved up at Caleb. He shouted, "You ready to go home?"

TOGETHER AGAIN

CALEB, SAM, AND OLFALA JOE made their way down-stream toward Joenriva. They moved slower going downstream than when Caleb and Sam had traveled upstream. Had it really been only one day ago? For Caleb, it felt as if a lifetime had passed in the last twenty-four hours. Olfala Joe set their pace now. It seemed that at every bend in the river, he needed to stop and share a story, a song, or a dance.

As they walked through the narrow slot canyon, Caleb heard a noise high above. Just a quick scraping sound, and then it was gone. Suddenly, a huge splash echoed through the canyon, and Sam and Olfala Joe both took off running. In the pool in front of them was a wild pig! It had fallen off the cliff above them, and it lay stunned in the water. Sam and Olfala Joe quickly grabbed it. Faster than Caleb could have ever believed possible, Olfala Joe whipped out a knife and slit the pig's throat. A long, high-pitched squeal bounced off the canyon walls, and then the pig lay limp. Olfala Joe smiled at Caleb. "Tunaet, yumi kakae pig!"

Caleb and Olfala Joe rested beside the pig while Sam searched for a big, sturdy branch they could use to carry it. When he returned, he and Joe used vines to truss the pig onto the branch. They carried it between them, with one end of the branch resting on Sam's shoulder and the other on Olfala Joe's. Burdened by the weight of the pig, they now moved even slower. On one hand, Caleb was thankful for the slow pace, as it kept him from tripping over stones. On the other hand, he knew Mom and Dad must be worried. He and Sam were supposed to have been gone for just a couple of hours. What must they have thought when he didn't return last night?

After what seemed like hours, the narrow canyon walls spread out, and Caleb could see Joenriva. He felt bad to leave Sam and Olfala Joe, but once the village was in sight, he desperately wanted to get back to Mom, Dad, and Anna. "Sam, I'm sorry, but I'm gonna go on ahead," he said. Sam and Olfala Joe both used their free hands to wave him on toward the village.

Caleb started to run now. Twice he stumbled; once he nearly face-planted. As he neared the village and the canyon grew wider, the stones were smaller, and the path became much easier to follow.

Suddenly, Caleb was sprinting up the clay bank that separated Joenriva from the Ora. He felt the waterproof bag holding the phone and satellite router slapping against his back as he ran toward the nurse's house and future medical clinic. "Mom! Dad! Anna! I'm home," he cried out.

Anna saw him coming up the path, turned, and yelled into the clinic. "Mom! Dad! Its Caleb! He's here!"

Anna ran down the steps of the clinic, barely feeling them beneath her feet. All night—that long, long night—she had prayed for Caleb, desperately trusting God to keep him safe and bring him back. Now here he was! Caleb was home! She grabbed him, buried her face in his shoulder, and held him tight. The tears that had been pent up all night long suddenly came flooding out.

Moments later, Anna felt Mom's arms go around her and Caleb, and then Daddy's strong arms wrapped around them all. It seemed as if everyone was crying at once. Anna heard Daddy whisper, "Thank you, Father. Thank you!"

CHANGES

June 28

AFTER THAT FATEFUL DAY when the river ran dry, the days began to blur together. Twice more, Caleb and Sam made the trek up the Ora to connect with the outside world. Once they went to summon Mr. Williams to carry the boy injured in the flash flood to the hospital in town. They had learned his name was Pita. The second time, they told Mr. Williams of the progress they were making on the clinic and passed news on to Granny and Grandpa Gristman and their friends at First Community Church. Each time, they brought back a host of emails and Facebook messages from back home and a brown burlap bag full of freshwater shrimp from the pool above the waterfall.

Joenriva had changed them all. They were leaner and suntanned. A stubble beard covered Mr. Gristman's jawline. Their hair seemed to be perpetually windblown—"beach hair," Anna called it. Their clothes showed the wear and tear of hand-washing in the river and sun-drying on the rocks. The carefully groomed Gristman family from America had been transformed by the harsh reality of jungle village life.

The changes on the inside were harder to express but went far deeper. Living without entertainment, internet access, or a busy schedule had drawn them much closer together as a family. Each evening, they played games and talked until inky darkness filled the world around them. Each morning, they shared a devotional time before starting the day's work.

Living in Joenriva had changed their perspective on life. Here, men and women worked all day just to provide enough food for the next day. Rather than focusing on gaining possessions or wealth, the people worked together to make sure everyone had enough to survive. The brush with death in the river had made them more aware of the precious and fragile nature of life. Here, life and community far outweighed things and money.

The biggest change was the friendships they had formed. Sam and Caleb had become nearly inseparable, as had Anna and Mari. And even though they struggled to understand him, the whole family had come to love Olfala Joe. Once they heard the story of how he had saved Caleb and Sam, they adopted him into the family. He had become a regular visitor, bringing them fruit and garden vegetables, a pet parrot, and on one occasion, a freshly killed fruit bat, which he insisted on giving them for their dinner. Comparing these friendships with the ones back home just didn't feel quite right. These friendships were forged in a different fire and had a different nature.

Now they were facing a big change as a family. Yesterday, they had finished painting the last room of the clinic. Mom and Anna gave the rooms one last cleaning before hanging the curtains. Dad and Caleb mounted the last solar panels and connected them to the battery bank. Today, the batteries would charge, and tomorrow, Mr. and Mrs. Williams—along with government representatives—would come from town and officially open the new clinic. An unwelcome change to their plans had transformed into an amazing and life-changing experience.

Anna stared into her hot chocolate and tried to sort out her feelings. She was glad the clinic was finished . . . excited that soon a missionary nurse would open the doors and begin to provide medical care to Joenriva and the surrounding communities. At the same time, she couldn't help but wonder what was next, and every time she thought of leaving Joenriva and Mari behind, a terrible lump swelled up in her throat.

"Mom, what will we do next?" Anna asked. "Will we go back to town and stay with the Williamses? We still have more than two weeks before we go back home."

"I'm not sure, Anna." Mom sighed wistfully. "I would enjoy a warm shower and a real bed."

"And a Coke," Caleb added. "And a burger and some fries! Right now, I would love one of Mrs. Williams' apple pies! Oh, and that roast chicken!"

Anna rolled her eyes. Of course, Caleb would be thinking about food.

Dad smiled as he worked on removing bits of paint stuck to his fingers. "Anna, do you remember how you and Caleb didn't want to come to Joenriva? Yet we've been part of making something amazing happen here, and I think we've all found it to be a home we never knew we had. I don't know what God has for us for the next two weeks, but I know we can trust him. Goodbyes are always hard, but for believers, it's really just 'See you later.'"

A BIG DAY

June 29

THE WHOLE VILLAGE bubbled with excitement. The women decorated the rooms of the clinic with fresh flowers. The men "planted" a thick forest of "trees" and vines in the yard of the clinic, blocking the path to the front door. For the first time since coming to Joenriva, Caleb, Anna, Mom, and Dad dressed up in their Sunday finest. Today was a big day . . . the biggest. Today, the mission clinic would officially open.

Later, a convoy of ten trucks, led by Mr. Williams' pickup, pulled into the village. Everyone gathered around and watched as the townsfolk poured out of the trucks. Anna chuckled in amusement as many of the government dignitaries reacted in shock to the villagers' lack of clothing. Just a short time ago, that had been her, she realized. Today, Joenriva just seemed like home. The people were friends. Thoughts about how they did or didn't dress had faded into the background.

The chief was dressed in his finest loincloth. He greeted the visitors and directed them to sit on some palm tree trunks that had been cut down just for this occasion. Fresh coconuts were brought and opened with great fanfare using a rusty machete. While the guests relaxed, some of the village women pulled Mrs. Williams aside and engaged in a noisy discussion. Anna couldn't understand what was being said, but she saw Mrs. Williams smile broadly and nod her head enthusiastically.

Soon the chief announced that it was time to begin. The sun beat down on the crowd. Mr. Williams made a speech. Two government officials made speeches.

Sweat trickled down Anna's back, and she began to wonder just how long they would talk. It would have been easier to endure if she could have understood what they were saying.

Finally, the chief stepped forward with his machete and boldly swept aside the "forest" of "trees" the men had put in place that morning. Holding out his machete, he invited the government officials and Mr. Williams to grasp the handle with him, and together they cut the last vine blocking the path. The clinic was open!

Inside, the dignitaries walked from room to room, nodding and exclaiming over the simple clinic. The people of Joenriva pressed in behind them, speaking rapidly in Tali and touching everything. Once the tour of the clinic was complete, everyone gathered in the shade of the covered porch that served as the clinic's waiting area. More coconuts were served, and Mr. Williams led the crowd in a short church service.

While Mr. Williams sang a simple worship song, Mom pulled on Anna's arm. "Anna, come with me." Together they slipped into the nurse's apartment.

Mom pulled out some of Anna's everyday clothes. "Here, change into these quickly."

Anna looked at her quizzically. Why on earth would Mom pull her away from the very first church service in Joenriva and ask her to change out of her church clothes? She started to ask but just shrugged and changed. Mom took her Sunday dress and folded it neatly.

"Go on back," she told Anna. "I'll join you in just a minute."

Anna made her way back to the service just as Mr. Williams put aside his guitar. He opened his Bible and began to preach. Everyone around Anna listened intently. She tried to listen, but she just couldn't understand. It was so hard to pay attention to a church service where she didn't understand the language.

Soon, Mr. Williams was wrapping up. He made an announcement that generated a surprised response from the crowd. Anna turned and looked at Mrs. Williams for an explanation. She smiled. "Today, we are not just opening a clinic. Today we are going to have the first baptism in Joenriva."

Everyone filed out of the clinic and gathered at the riverside next to one of Anna's favorite swimming spots. Mr. Williams played his guitar and sang another song, and then he taught a short lesson about water baptism—what it is and why Christians get baptized.

Mrs. Williams tugged on Anna's sleeve. "Look," she whispered, pointing up the path toward the village. Coming down the path were Mari, her mother, her father, and two of her brothers. The whole family was wearing clothes—and Mari was wearing Anna's Sunday dress!

Mari's father stood before the crowd and began to speak. Mrs. Williams, standing between Anna and Mom, translated for them. "For many years, I have been searching. I have tried to follow the teaching of my fathers, but I knew in my heart that something was missing. When this family came to Joenriva, I saw that they were different. I saw the love they had for one another. I watched their children and saw that they were obedient and respectful. They were kind and loving toward everyone they met. I asked myself, 'What makes them different? What do they have that

I do not?' I asked the missionary, and he told me it was Jesus. On the day the river ran dry, I saw how this Jesus gave them peace. I watched my Mari. I saw how after they prayed with her, she too had peace. I told my wife, 'It is time. We will follow this Jesus.'"

Anna watched as, one by one, they stepped into the river and were baptized. Mari was last. She came out of the water with a smile so big it made her whole face shine. Anna felt as if her heart would burst.

Mrs. Williams pulled Anna close. "Remember your first day here, when you said you felt like you didn't have anything to do? I encouraged you to focus on being—being a good friend and a godly young woman." Anna nodded, her eyes bright. "You did it, Anna," Mrs. Williams said, giving her a squeeze. "You did it very well. And because you did, Mari and her family have begun to follow Jesus."

Later, over lunch, Caleb asked Mr. Williams what was next. Mr. Williams smiled. "Well," he said, "If I remember right, two young people wanted to see the homestead of pioneer missionary J. Noble MacKenzie. Tomorrow morning, we'll drive down to the ocean. I've scheduled a boat to take us to Hakua."

HAKUA

EARLY THE NEXT MORNING, the Gristmans packed their bags and loaded them in Mr. Williams' truck. The entire village gathered to see them off. The men shook each of their hands. The women kissed their cheeks, gave them hugs, and wiped away more than a few tears. Anna looked around for Mari. Where was she? Surely she wouldn't miss the opportunity to say goodbye. Anna felt all mixed up inside—excited about finally going to see the west coast and like crying every time she thought about leaving Mari behind.

Just then, Mari and Sam joined the crowd around the truck. Sam reached out and shook Caleb's hand. It looked like he was struggling to control his emotions. Yesterday, when Mari had been baptized, Caleb had watched Sam. Sam had been biting his lip to keep his face from showing his emotions, just as he had back in the cave with Olfala Joe. Caleb realized that Sam was torn between following Christ and following the example of his uncle, the Tali chief.

On a whim, Caleb reached into his bag, pulled out his best shirt, and offered it to Sam. "Here, take this so you can remember our adventures together."

Anna hugged Mari tight. Both of them cried a little. How could you be best friends with someone when you couldn't even speak their language? Anna wondered. Would she ever see Mari again? Anna was so thankful that Mari had trusted in Jesus. Now she knew that one day, she and Mari would be together in heaven. She knew too that she would carry Mari and Joenriva in her heart forever.

Once all the goodbyes had been said, the family piled into the truck for a two-hour ride. The thick tangle of vines they drove past was broken occasionally by a clearing for a small village. At each village, naked children froze in astonishment and stared at them as they drove past. Caleb and Anna would wave and smile, and the children, as if waking from a trance, would smile, wave, and race behind the truck, shouting, until they disappeared in a cloud of dust.

At last, the thick jungle ended, and the truck pulled up in the shade of a massive banyan tree. Caleb and Anna stared up in awe at its thick tangle of branches, roots, and vines. It was hard to believe that one tree could be so huge. Just beyond the banyan, a black-sand beach stretched down to sparkling water. Together, Caleb and Anna ran out onto the beach. For miles up and down the coast, black sand, fringed with palm trees and banyans, lined the seashore.

There, in the ocean before them, a small aluminum boat bobbed gently on the waves. A young boy sitting on the side of the boat waved at them before jumping into the surf and guiding the boat to the shore. "Kam!" he cried, motioning them toward the boat.

Caleb scrambled on board. "Oh wow! This is going to be awesome!"

Soon their luggage, Mom and Dad, and Mr. and Mrs. Williams were all loaded onto the boat. The captain came out of the shade of the banyan tree carrying two large tanks of fuel, and they pulled away from the shore.

At Mr. Williams' insistence, Caleb and Anna climbed up onto the roof of the boat and faced the oncoming waves. It felt a little bit like flying, as the boat dipped into the troughs and bobbed over the crests. The wind blew their hair and chased away the heat of the sun. Mr. Williams pulled a spool of heavy fishing line out of his backpack, tied on a lure, and peeled off fifty feet of line before passing the spool over to Mr. Gristman. "Let's see if you can catch us some supper!"

. The boy who had welcomed them onto the boat joined them on the roof. He pointed at his chest, "Nem blong mi Jon."

"I'm Caleb, and this is Anna," Caleb responded.

"Caleb . . . Anna," Jon repeated. "Yu likim dolfen? Traem kilim boat, olsem." With that, Jon began to slap his palm against the boat rhythmically. Caleb and Anna joined him.

"Luk! Dolfen."

Anna squealed in amazement as a pair of dolphins joined them on each side of the boat. It was amazing to watch as they shot through the water and leapt into the air.

"Wow! How cool is this?" Caleb asked.

After the dolphins slipped away, Caleb and Anna began to tire of the ride. Other than the occasional flying fish, everything looked the same. Far to their left, a finger of dark mountains looked black on the horizon. Pointing to where the mountains disappeared into the sea far to the north, Caleb asked Jon, "Hakua?" Jon just shook his head no.

Splashing a bit of water onto the roof of the boat, Jon drew a wavy line that doubled back on itself. Caleb realized that he was drawing a map of the western peninsula of Santo. Jon pointed to a spot a third of the way up the line and then pointed back to where the mountains disappeared into the sea. "That, close; Hakua long way, very long way. Tudak mi ting."

Caleb looked to Mr. Williams for clarification. "What you are seeing is Pisina," Mr. Williams explained. "It's a point that juts out from the shore about a third of the way up the peninsula. It will be dark before we get to Hakua."

Caleb and Anna both felt numb when they finally reached the tip of the western peninsula just at sunset. Here, the jagged mountains slumped into the sea, the land ended, and they turned west into the setting sun. The glassy, calm water brilliantly

reflected the oranges and reds of the sky. Seabirds cried as they swirled, dove, and dipped into the water.

Suddenly, the fishing line in Dad's hand went taut. The captain idled the engine while Dad and Mr. Williams wrestled a fat tuna aboard. "Great job!" Mr. Williams exulted. "I knew you would catch our dinner!"

The sun slowly slipped behind the waves, and stars began to sparkle across a velvet sky. It was just dark enough to spot a single kerosene lantern glowing on the shore. The captain carefully guided the boat into a narrow channel between two massive slabs of stone. At last, they slid into a neat, round, natural harbor. Mrs. Williams looked up at them with a weary smile. "We're here. Welcome to Hakua."

DIGNITY

CALEB COULD BARELY keep his eyes open as the women of Hakua prepared the tuna Dad had caught. When it was finally ready, he feasted on the fresh tuna, baked sweet potatoes, ripe papaya, bananas, and grapefruit. It was a treat after all the canned food they had eaten at Joenriva.

As soon as supper was finished, they headed off to bed. As they were going, Mr. Williams told him, "Tomorrow we'll hike up to the MacKenzie homestead, and you can hear the story of Mrs. MacKenzie's candle."

As Caleb lay down on his camping mat, he wondered briefly what Mr. Williams meant. But the moment his eyes closed, he fell deeply asleep.

Early the next morning, Caleb woke to the sound of dozens of roosters. It was as if they were competing to be first to announce the sunrise. He was eager to see Hakua in the daylight. Stepping out into the sunlight, he was amazed at the difference between

Hakua and Joenriva. Here, each home was made of thatch and bamboo, as in Joenriva. But instead of being low and dark, they had windows with delicate latticework screens and colorful curtains. Each yard was carefully groomed and neatly hedged by flowers or bushes with brightly colored leaves. Hens led broods of chicks down the carefully swept walkways, and roosters strutted and crowed. But there were no pigs rooting around the houses.

The men he saw were dressed in shorts and brightly colored shirts, and the women wore flowing dresses in cheerful floral patterns. The children were clean and sported smart school uniforms. As he stepped into the kitchen, where Mom and Dad were drinking coffee with Mr. and Mrs. Williams, Caleb was greeted by the smell of frying eggs. A table with a bright floral tablecloth was set with plates, glasses, and silverware. Platters heaped with sliced pineapple, bananas, grapefruit, papaya, and homemade bread lined the table.

He was a bit confused. When he had gotten used to Joenriva, he thought he understood Vanuatu—or at least what village life was like in Vanuatu. Yet this was completely different from Joenriva. What made the difference? He was about to ask Mr. Williams when he realized that this was exactly what they were talking about.

"It's about dignity." Mr. Williams was saying. "All of humanity carries the image of God. Satan hates that image. Whenever people live without the knowledge of the gospel, they are living under his control. Satan does everything he can to strip people of their dignity. Whenever you visit a pre-Christian village, you'll find that it's dirty. There's hardly ever any grass. The pigs are allowed to eat from the same dishes as the children, and diseases and sores are common."

"Yes, we saw that at Joenriva," Mom said. "But this is so different. It must take a lot of teaching to see this kind of change."

"Actually, no," Mrs. Williams responded. "When people come to know Christ, he restores their dignity. You don't have to teach them to clean up their yards, homes, or even themselves and their children. No one has to teach them to put their pigs in pens and keep them out of their homes. I'm convinced that it's the Holy Spirit working in their lives that makes the difference. It's always amazing to watch the change that happens as people are brought into relationship with God."

"We've seen the same thing in America," Dad agreed. "Whenever we visit the home of an alcoholic or drug addict, we're always shocked at how filthy their homes are and how often they and their children are unwashed and wearing dirty clothes. Yet, as soon as they find Christ and are delivered, it's amazing how fast they clean up."

"That's it," Mr. Williams responded. "Really, we're talking about two kingdoms—the Kingdom of Light and the Kingdom of Darkness. Our lives reflect the kingdom we belong to."

There was a pause in the conversation as the adults picked up their cups and thoughtfully sipped their coffee. Just then, Caleb remembered Mr. Williams' comment from the night before. "Mr. Williams," Caleb said. "Will you tell me the story of Mrs. MacKenzie's candle?"

Mr. Williams smiled kindly. "That story isn't mine to tell," he said. "You'll have to wait for Pastor Jon."

MRS. MACKENZIE'S CANDLE

AS THEY FINISHED BREAKFAST, a short, heavyset man with salt-and-pepper hair slipped through the door and sat down heavily in a chair at the end of the table. His breath had a raspy sound that reminded Caleb of when his best friend back home had an asthma attack. The man reached for a slice of buttered bread, and one of the women brought him a massive cup of hot tea. He took a large bite, chewed slowly, drank deeply of the tea, and then sat back in his chair and smiled at them. "Welcome to Hakua. I am Pastor Jon."

Pastor Jon studied the children intently. "So, you want to visit the MacKenzie homestead?" he asked. They both nodded eagerly. After a long, expectant pause, Pastor Jon continued. "You need to understand that J. Noble MacKenzie and his wife are very important to us here in Hakua. You see, when our grandfathers where in darkness, the MacKenzies came and lived among us. They were the first ever to bring the gospel to these shores."

Caleb couldn't keep from interrupting. "I read that you can still see the path he made as he traveled between Hakua and Nukuku on horseback, preaching the gospel in each of the villages."

"That's right," Pastor Jon confirmed. "Today I will show you that path. MacKenzie not only preached the gospel, but he translated the Bible into our language. He wrote many hymns in our language and helped us establish the very first churches in our tribe."

"What about Mrs. MacKenzie," Anna asked softly. "What did she do?"

Pastor Jon's face grew somber. "Sadly, Mrs. MacKenzie contracted malaria and died," he said reverently. "She is buried at Nukuku. But before she died, she lit a candle that changed our tribe forever."

"That's what you were talking about!" Caleb said to Mr. Williams. "I can't wait to hear about her candle."

Pastor Jon laughed, "Well, you will need to wait just a bit longer. Let me finish my tea, and then we can hike up to their homestead."

Once Pastor Jon had finished his tea, Caleb, Anna, and Dad followed him though the village and began to climb the hill. "Missionary MacKenzie intended to build his house at the top the hill so that he could see ships as they came into the harbor. However, he had a problem: there was no source of water on top of the hill. So he ordered a large iron tank and brought it with him.

"When he arrived, he convinced the chief of Hakua to have his men help him carry the tank to the top of the hill. My great-grandfather was one of the men who helped. It was a very heavy tank. As they climbed the hill with the tank, my great-grandfather asked the chief in the Hakua language if, instead of carrying the heavy tank up the hill, they could kill the missionary and eat him. The chief agreed, and they planned to kill and eat the MacKenzies, but not while they were awake. He was afraid that Mr. MacKenzie might have a weapon they didn't know about. 'Wait until they go to sleep,' the chief told his men. 'Then you can kill them, and we can all eat them tomorrow.'"

Pastor Jon stopped and pointed to a deep rut in the hillside. "See that? That is the path MacKenzie made with his horse. It was the very first horse we had ever seen."

"Oh, wow!" Caleb said enthusiastically. "Pastor Jon, you have to take a picture of us walking down the path that MacKenzie made."

As Pastor Jon took their picture, he remarked, "You are standing on the path that carried the gospel to my people."

As they started back up the hillside, Anna asked, "So, if the chief agreed that your great-grandfather and his friends should kill the MacKenzies that first night, what happened? How were they able to share the gospel?"

Pastor Jon smiled. "Mrs. MacKenzie lit a candle."

"Okay, now you have to tell us the story," Anna pleaded.

"Not until we get to Mrs. MacKenzie's kitchen," Pastor Jon replied.

As they neared the top of the hill, they came to a low stone wall. "See this," Pastor Jon said, gesturing toward it. "This is the wall that MacKenzie built around his yard. Once you step over this wall, you are in the MacKenzie homestead."

Together, they followed the low wall around the homestead, and Caleb marked out the corners on a GPS app he had downloaded just for this purpose. From then on, there would be a clear record of the exact location of the MacKenzie homestead. Caleb planned on using this for a history report next year.

Pastor Jon then led them to a large hole in the center of the yard. "This was their cellar for storing food. The house is completely gone, but if you look around, you might find some of their things."

Caleb, Anna, and Dad began combing through the thick grass. "I found something," Anna shouted. There in the grass were the rusted remains of a cast iron cookstove.

"Just think," Dad said. "When Mr. MacKenzie would come back from a long trip on horseback, Mrs. MacKenzie would have hot coffee or tea waiting for him on this very stove top."

A few minutes later, Caleb found the rusted remains of the water tank Pastor Jon's great-grandfather had helped carry up the hill. Pastor Jon reached out and touched it. "The last time someone from my family touched this tank, they were making a plan to kill and eat the missionary. What an amazing difference the gospel makes! Now come over here where the kitchen was, and I will tell you the story of Mrs. MacKenzie's candle."

As they gathered around Pastor Jon in the MacKenzies' kitchen, Caleb noticed that Dad looked almost as eager to hear the story as Caleb felt. They had waited a long time for this. Pastor Jon continued the story in a low, conspiratorial tone. "That night, my great-grandfather and his friends crept into the bushes around the MacKenzie home and waited for the MacKenzies to go to sleep. 'How will we know when they are asleep?' they asked each other. They decided they would wait until the MacKenzies' cooking fire went out. Then they would attack.

"As Mr. and Mrs. MacKenzie prepared to go to bed, Mrs. MacKenzie stepped into the kitchen, lit a candle, and placed it on the table. Then they went to sleep. My great-grandfather and his friends had never seen a candle before. So they thought the light they saw was from the cooking fire. They waited and waited, but the candle kept burning. The men were tired from carrying the heavy tank up the hill. They finally decided to go home, get some sleep, and come back and kill the MacKenzies the following night.

"Night after night, they crept through the bushes and laid in ambush for the MacKenzies. Night after night, Mrs. MacKenzie would step into the kitchen, light a candle, and place it on the table. Finally, convinced that the MacKenzies never slept, my great-grandfather abandoned his plan to kill them. He listened to the message they had brought, and he became the first believer in our tribe. Only after he became a believer did he learn about candles and understand why the light from Mrs. MacKenzie's 'cooking fire' never went out.

"You see, Mrs. MacKenzie lit a candle. Without her knowing it, her light saved the MacKenzies' lives, and it allowed the light of the gospel to change my tribe."

There was a reverent silence as the listeners enjoyed the story's satisfying message and let its importance sink in fully. "Caleb, Anna, I have one request of you," Pastor Jon concluded. "Find a dark place in this world . . . and light a candle."

HOME

FOR THE NEXT TWO WEEKS, the Gristman family and Mr. and Mrs. Williams slowly made their way down the west coast of Santo. Each day, they stopped at a new village and held an evangelistic service. Each night, many people responded to the call to put their faith in Jesus. Night after night, village chiefs and church elders thanked them for coming.

All too soon, they were standing at the tiny airport outside Luganville. The night before they left, Anna had emptied her suitcases of all but two outfits and carried them to Mrs. Williams. Tearfully, she asked her to take them to Mari the next time they went to Big Bay. Mrs. Williams had given her a big hug. Although she didn't say anything, Anna knew that Mrs. Williams understood how she felt.

Now, standing at the airport, she could tell that they all felt torn about leaving. Who knew you could fall in love with a place in just two months? Who knew you could make friends who would change your life? At the end of that plane ride, Granny and Grandpa Gristman would be waiting. Their friends and church family would be waiting. But on this side of the of the plane ride were Mari, Sam, Olfala Joe, and Pastor Jon.

A big Boeing jet, painted brightly in the colors of Vanuatu's flag—red, green, black, and yellow— landed and taxied to the tiny terminal. The noise of its engines drowned out all conversation. It seemed to Anna that the airport was the point of contact between two very different worlds. Here, the Tali lived hidden away in the jungle, their lives untouched by the modern world. There, starting in the plane, was a modern world. That world was clean, neat, and comfortable. Standing on the threshold between the worlds, Anna wondered for a moment which one she belonged to. In a flash, she realized that she didn't belong to either world. Her home was heaven.

The noise of the plane's engine slowly died away, and they stood watching a curious mixture of wide-eyed tourists and local travelers disembark. With their eyes fixed on the plane, they failed to see Sam approaching them. He seemed to just suddenly appear at Caleb's side.

At first, Sam stood silently. Then he reached into the woven pandanas basket hanging at his side and pulled out a large, strange-looking tooth. It curved around until the sharp tip of the tooth nearly touched its root. Sam held it out to Caleb.

"This is a pig's tusk," Sam told him. "It is our traditional money in Vanuatu. My grandfather grew this pig. He raised it very carefully so that the tusk wouldn't break. When it was time for my father to become a man, Grandfather killed the pig for a feast and gave this tusk to my father. My father gave it to me. Now, I want you to have it. I want you to take it back to America and remember me and my family.

You've been a good friend, Caleb. I will remember what you said about Jesus."

Anna watched the two of them. Caleb shuffled his feet and sniffed a couple of times before reaching out to accept the pig's tusk and awkwardly shake hands with Sam. Anna knew he was trying to think of what he could give Sam in return.

Sam turned to go. "Wait!" Caleb said, "I want you to have my phone. Mr. Williams can show you how to set it up in your name and use it. Then you and I can connect online. You'll help him, won't you, Mr.

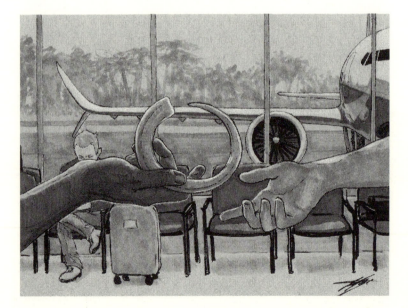

Williams?" Caleb quickly dug the charging cord out of his backpack and handed it and the phone over to Sam.

Just then, the loudspeaker made an indecipherable racket. "That will be you," Mr. Williams said, squeezing Caleb's shoulder fondly.

There was one more flurry of hugs all around before Caleb and Anna walked across the hot tarmac and climbed the stairs to board the plane. The flight attendant greeted them with a wide smile, and they stepped into air conditioning for the first time in a long time.

They were going home.

A note from the author

I and my family have lived in Vanuatu for the last twenty years. Vanuatu is very much our home. I am excited to share a story about the people and place I love through the eyes of Caleb and Anna. I have modified tribal names, invented places and moved things around to help with the flow of the story and to protect the privacy of my island friends. All profits from the sale of Mrs. MacKenzie's Candle *will be used to help children like Sam and Mari know about Jesus.*